Text copyright © 1990 Maryann Macdonald
Illustration copyright © 1990 Judith Riches

First published 1990 by ABC
33 Museum Street, London WC1A 1LD

Printed and bound in Hong Kong
by Imago Services (HK) Ltd.

All rights reserved.

Sam's Worries

WRITTEN BY **Maryann Macdonald**

ILLUSTRATED BY **Judith Riches**

Hyperion Books for Children

One night, Sam couldn't go to sleep. He was worried.

He was worried that there might be a volcano under his house.

He was worried that there were cobras in his garage.

He was worried that there could be an earthquake while he was at school.

He was worried that the lunchroom lady was a witch.

He was worried that he would lose
his library books.

He was worried about vampires
and monsters and bogeymen.

And he was worried that he wouldn't go to heaven because he often stole cookies from the cookie jar.

Mom didn't think he needed to worry about these things.

"There has never been a volcano here," she said, "or an earthquake. And cobras live in India."

"Mrs. Sparks may look a little creepy, but she is not a witch. Your library books are in a stack on the piano. And vampires and monsters and bogeymen don't exist."

Sam had not told her about the cookies.

Mom kissed Sam and tucked him in again. "Now
go to sleep, sweetheart," she said, "and stop worrying."
She turned off the light and went downstairs.

But Sam could not stop worrying. "Maybe there's never been a volcano or an earthquake here before, but there is always a first time," he whispered to his bear.

"Right," said the bear. "And cobras might swim here from India."

"Yes," said Sam, "they might. And Mrs. Sparks might be just pretending to be a nice lady."

The bear nodded. "To fool mothers," he said.

"Yes," said Sam.

"Just because your library books are on the piano, doesn't mean you'll remember them," said the bear.

"No," agreed Sam, "and I could lose one on the way to the library."

"You could," said the bear. "And if vampires and monsters and bogeymen don't exist, why are so many people afraid of them?"

Sam sighed. "Mothers don't know everything."

"They don't," said the bear. "And I know how you feel about the cookies. I'm a cookie thief myself."

Sam felt better. His bear understood. But he was still worried.

"Tell you what," said the bear. "I will worry about the cobras and the earthquakes and everything while you sleep."

"Will you?" said Sam.

"Sure," said the bear. "Then you can worry about them in the daytime while I sleep."

"Okay," said Sam. And Sam closed his eyes, snuggled
into his soft pillow and drifted away to sleep.

The bear stayed awake all night worrying.

In the morning, Sam felt fine. "Good old bear," he said, and he took the bear and put his head on his own soft pillow and tucked him gently under the covers.

Then he went downstairs and ate his breakfast and decided not to worry about cobras and earthquakes. They did not seem so worrying when the sun was shining.

And the bear slept soundly all day anyway.